Scholastic's The Magic School Bus

IN THE HAUNTED MUSEUM
A Book About Sound

From an episode of the animated TV series
produced by Scholastic Productions, Inc.
Based on *The Magic School Bus* books
written by Joanna Cole and illustrated by Bruce Degen

SCHOLASTIC INC.
New York Toronto London Auckland Sydney

TV tie-in book adaptation by Linda Ward Beech
and illustrated by Joel Schick.
TV script written by John May,
Kristin Laskas Martin, and Jocelyn Stevenson.

Library of Congress Cataloging-in-Publication Data

Beech, Linda,
Scholastic's The magic school bus in the haunted museum:
a book about sound / from an episode of the animated TV series produced by Scholastic Productions,
Inc.; based on the Magic school bus books written by
Joanna Cole and illustrated by Bruce Degen.
p.   cm.
"TV tie-in book adaptation by Linda Ward Beech and illustrated by Joel Schick,
TV script written by John May, Kristin Laskas Martin,
and Jocelyn Stevenson"—T.p. verso.
ISBN 0-590-48412-5
1. Sound—Juvenile literature.   2. Science museums—Educational aspects—
Juvenile literature. [1. Sound.   2. Music—Acoustics and physics.   3. Musical instruments.]   I.
Cole, Joanna.   II. Schick, Joel, ill.   III. Scholastic Productions.   IV. Title.   V. Title: Magic school
bus in the haunted museum.
QC225.5.B37   1995   94-25970
534—dc20   CIP   AC

302928   0100

Printed in the U.S.A.   23

First Scholastic printing, January 1995

In Ms. Frizzle's class we were getting ready for our concert at the Sound Museum. But something was wrong. It was the instrument that Carlos had made. It *looked* terrific, but as Ralphie said, it sounded "ploopy." How could we play "Concerto for Invented Instrument" with a ploopy sound?

Ms. Frizzle was the only one who didn't seem worried. She encouraged Carlos by saying, "Just keep asking questions and you'll keep getting answers!" Then she hustled us onto the school bus. We were late for the dress rehearsal of our concert. We had to get to the Sound Museum in a hurry.

During the ride Carlos worked on his instrument.
"I don't think it's getting better," said Dorothy Ann.
"He needs more time," agreed Tim.
That's when the bus began to act strangely. This happens
a lot when the Friz is driving.

While we pushed, Carlos kept working. His instrument looked better and better. It sounded worse and worse. Meanwhile, we kept hearing all these *spooky* sounds.

Then, we heard a different sound. Ms. Friz called it "mellifluous." It was also coming from the old creepy house.

We wanted to get back on the bus, but the Friz cried, "Take chances! Make mistakes!"

Then, she rang the doorbell. Boy, did it sound off!

Carlos heard the amazing sound, too.

"Listen to that! I need to find out what's making that sound," said Carlos.

"I *knew* I should have stayed home today," Arnold said.

When the door swung open, Carlos and Ms. Frizzle walked right in. The rest of the class followed.

"Helloo-ooo-ooo," called Ms. Frizzle.

"Helloo-ooo-ooo," her voice echoed back to us.

No one greeted us. The door swung shut, and it wouldn't open. We were stuck in the house!

"Here's a phone book," said Dorothy Ann. "Maybe we can call for help."

But, when Dorothy Ann opened that phone book, it rang! The Friz opened other books. We heard foghorns, roars, whispers, screams, and some crazy laughter. The books were filled with sounds!

"I wonder who lives here," said Keesha nervously.

Then Ms. Frizzle told us about the owner, Professor Cornelia C. Contralto. "Cornelia was an eccentric collector of sounds," she explained. "She disappeared about a hundred years ago."

We weren't surprised. Who would want to live in this house?

"Class," said the Friz, "this house is actually the Sound Museum."

That did surprise us—especially since the museum was closed for the night. And we were in it!

"We have the whole place to ourselves," said Ms. Frizzle. "Great!" said Carlos.

Not everyone was so happy. Ralphie was worried about Professor Cornelia C. Contralto. "I bet she's a ghost," he said. "Maybe she's in the house seeking the perfect sound."

This was an interesting thought. The house was full of surprising sounds.

CREEAK!

It was time for bed. The museum just happened to have enough kid-sized beds for everyone. We got *way* under the covers. Carlos was still thinking about his instrument. So far nothing had improved it.

"Cornelia, if you're out there, will you help me make this thing sound right?" he called.

We heard that sound again! Someone or something had answered Carlos. He ran from the room to see what it was. We scrambled after Carlos. Before we could stop him, he had opened a door . . .

. . . and we were in a strange room. Every time we turned around, we saw something different. We ran from a jungle to the mountains. Ms. Frizzle was there, yodeling. Her yodel bounced from one mountain to another. It was an echo.

YODEL-AY-EE-OO!

YODEL-AY-EE-OO!

Once is enough!

From there we tumbled into the Giant Room. It was full of gigantic musical instruments. Dorothy Ann pulled the string of a harp. The string moved back and forth and made a musical sound.

Ms. Frizzle said, "That movement is a vibration."

Keesha added, "When the string stops vibrating, the sound stops."

Carlos asked, "Are all sounds made by something vibrating?"

It didn't take long to find out. Tim and Phoebe played the drum by making it vibrate. Wanda rang the gong by making it vibrate. They not only heard the sound, they felt it, too!

Then Ms. Frizzle rang a giant bell. The vibrations filled the room. Suddenly the wall cracked open. We followed the Friz through the wall and onto a stage.

Ms. Frizzle gave Carlos some funny-looking glasses. They must have been magic. They let Carlos *see* sound waves!

"Sound waves look like the ripples in a pond," he cried. "They're circles within circles, moving outward."

Look! He's talking in circles!

We all put on magic glasses. It was fun making sounds and watching the vibrations. The sound waves started in one place and moved out in all directions.

Ms. Frizzle showed us something else. First, she sang a high note. The circles came out close together. Next, she sang a low note. The circles were farther apart.

"Class," said the Friz, "high sounds are made when something vibrates fast. Low sounds are made by something vibrating more slowly."

Then Carlos got a really soundproof idea. "It doesn't matter how my instrument *looks*. What matters is how it *vibrates*."

He dashed back to the bedroom. His instrument was gone!

We were nervous. We heard that amazing sound again. Then the lights went out.

"That sound is coming from the closet door!" cried Dorothy Ann.

Carlos opened the door — and disappeared. He had fallen into a dungeon!

That didn't bother the Friz. She jumped right in, too, and shouted, "Follow me, kids!"

This seemed like an unsound idea, but she was our teacher. ARGGGGH! Soon we were all down there together.

The sound was bouncing off the walls of the long hallway. We followed the sound waves around the corner to the end of the hall.

The sounds were coming through a door. Carlos opened it. Inside we saw someone sitting at an organ. It was Cornelia C. Contralto, the third! The original Cornelia had been her great-grandmother. From behind the organ, Cornelia pulled out Carlos's instrument.

Hmmmm. That strikes a familiar note.

Carlos knew exactly what to do. He began taking things off the instrument. "With so much stuff on it, the instrument can't vibrate the way it needs to," he explained.

We gave a terrific concert! Everyone loved the amazing sounds from Carlos's invented instrument. Cornelia liked them so much, she asked for the instrument. She said no Sound Museum was complete without it. She was right!

A Funny Phone Call

Uh-oh! There's that phony phone ringing again. Who could it be?

Magic School Bus: Hello?

Caller: I think your imagination got away with you in this book.

Magic School Bus: What do you mean? Everything in the book is true.

Caller: Well, that doorbell can't be real.

Magic School Bus: Mmmm, maybe you're right. But it's a great idea!

Caller: You don't expect readers to believe that books can make all those sounds, do you?

Magic School Bus: You're right. That's make-believe.

Caller: And you can't really see sound, can you?

Magic School Bus: No. That's why the kids wore magic glasses. But everything else in the book is true.

Caller: What about the ghost? There aren't really any ghosts.

Magic School Bus: No, of course not.

Caller: And I don't think school buses are magical either.

Magic School Bus: No, they're not. But I bet you wish they were. Just use your imagination!

From the desk of Ms. Frizzle

Take Chances! Make mistakes!

Sound begins when something moves or vibrates. Stretch several rubber bands of different thicknesses around a book. Which makes a higher sound, a thick band or a thin one? Try playing music on your rubber-band instrument.

Sound vibrations travel as waves. Drop a penny in a pan of water. The ripples you see are like sound waves. Like the ripples, sound waves move away from their source. Find the sound waves in this book. Where are they going?

Ears catch sound. The brain makes it meaningful. Sounds help people communicate. Listen to the sounds around you. Make sounds by speaking or singing. Look for the ways that Ms. Frizzle and the kids make sounds in this book.

Some animals use sound to help them. Bats can't see well, but they use echoes to help them get around. Find the bats in the book.

You can direct sound. Speak into a tube or cup your hands around your mouth. The sound waves are squeezed into the tube so they don't spread out as quickly. Find some instruments in the book that direct sound.

Ms. Frizzle